Journey to Mars

Journey to
MARS

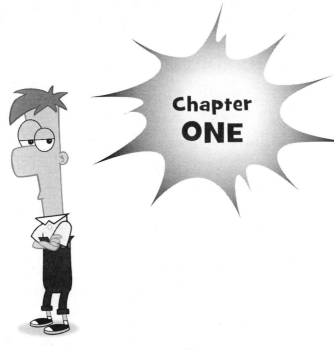

Phineas Flynn and Ferb Fletcher were sprawled under a tree in their backyard as sunlight streamed through the leaves over-head. It was another fun day of summer vacation, and all the boys had to do was figure out how to spend it! Ever since they had vowed to have the best summer ever, Phineas and Ferb's days had been filled with one adventure after another. Phineas and Ferb

3

weren't just stepbrothers—they were also best friends! And from Phineas's nonstop ideas to Ferb's exceptional building skills, they made a great team . . . especially when it came time to plan each day's activities. In fact, Phineas and Ferb had so many excellent ideas they'd started to keep track of them all in a list on their laptop.

"What should we do today?" Phineas asked as he scrolled through the list. "Build an underwater skate park? Sounds pretty wicked! Fly with rocket-powered bat wings? Awesome! Teach Perry tricks?"

Phineas paused to look down at his pet platypus, Perry, who was perched nearby. "He's just a platypus. He doesn't do much," Phineas said, shrugging his shoulders.

Perry started chattering in response, making a cute little platypus noise that seemed to confirm what Phineas had said. But in reality, Perry was a secret operative known as Agent P!

He worked for O.W.C.A. or, Organization Without a Cool Acronym. O.W.C.A. was dedicated to identifying and fighting evil in all its forms, and because of the sensitive nature of these secret activities, O.W.C.A. agents went deep undercover. Years of training had turned Agent P into one of the smartest, most skilled platypuses on the planet—but only a few people in the world knew that. And to protect Agent P's secret identity, Phineas and Ferb were not among them.

Before Phineas could get back to reading through his list, a visitor arrived in the backyard. It was Isabella Garcia-Shapiro, leader of the local Fireside Girls troop and one of Phineas's and Ferb's best friends and neighbors.

"Oh, hi, Isabella!" Phineas exclaimed.

"Hey, Phineas, you might want to go check up on Baljeet," Isabella said with a worried look on her face. "I was walking by his house and heard him scream, 'Ay-eee! I'm doomed to be an incompetent flunky forever . . . ever . . . ever . . . ever . . .'" Isabella let her voice trail off. "I added the echo part," she said.

Phineas and Ferb were already on their feet, and Perry jumped up, too. "Sounds pretty serious," Phineas said as he grabbed his computer. Then he and Ferb hurried out to the sidewalk, thinking Perry was trailing behind them. But they were wrong. Perry had important spy business to attend to.

Their friend Baljeet Rai lived just a few blocks away. "Baljeet! It's Phineas and Ferb!" Phineas called as he and Ferb walked into Baljeet's house. They hurried down the hall to his bedroom, which was dark and gloomy. "Why are all the lights off?" Phineas asked.

Sitting in the shadows, Baljeet didn't even look up. "Darkness is a shroud that hides my shame," he said sadly. Then he buried his face in his hands.

"Hey, buddy. Why don't you tell us what's going on?" Phineas asked in concern.

"Because of the seventeen summer school classes I am taking, I qualified for the science fair," Baljeet explained. He unrolled a stack of papers. "So, I decided to design this."

Phineas and Ferb glanced at the papers and realized that they were blueprints. "A portal to Mars? Cool!" Phineas exclaimed.

"No! *Not* cool," Baljeet replied, grabbing the blueprints and rolling them back up. "When I showed my teacher, he said . . ." Baljeet closed his eyes at the memory.

He could still hear the disbelief in Mr. McGillicuddy's voice when he asked, "A portal to Mars? And . . . what does it do?"

"Well, without overcomplicating things, it's a . . . portal to Mars," Baljeet told his teacher. "You step through it, and you're on Mars."

"Well, this is very creative," began Mr. McGillicuddy, "but unless you can build a working model, the best I could give you is—"

"An A-minus!" Baljeet howled to Phineas

and Ferb as he crumpled the blueprints into a ball. "That would be the worst grade of my life!"

Phineas didn't quite understand the problem. "Why won't you just build one?" he asked.

"I am not mechanically inclined like the two of you," Baljeet moaned.

"I know what we're going to do today!" Phineas announced. "Baljeet, we'll help you build the portal!"

"Good," Baljeet said, cheering up at once.

"With your mechanical inclinations and my scientific expertise, we are a team that cannot be beaten—"

"Wait," Phineas interrupted him, glancing around. "Where's Perry?"

Baljeet and Ferb looked around, too, but they didn't see Perry anywhere. "Did you have him when you came over?" Baljeet asked.

Phineas shrugged. He was sure Perry was around somewhere. But for now, they had work to do!

As soon as Phineas and Ferb left their house, Perry slipped away to a file cabinet that doubled as an entrance to his secret lair. Slapping a fedora on his head, Perry transformed into Agent P and plunged through the passageway. He landed in the large captain's chair where he received orders from Major Monogram, the commander of the spy agency. He sat there while papers from the file cabinet drifted around him.

Major Monogram was in the middle of adjusting his buzz-cut–style toupee when Agent P arrived. He cleared his throat awkwardly as he gave his hairpiece one last tug. "Oh, uh, Agent P, it appears that Dr. Doofenshmirtz has made some rather unusual purchases: chicken wire, three metric tons of baking soda, and lederhosen. You know, those bib-front leather shorts that make you look like a walking cuckoo clock?" Major Monogram shook his head in horror. "Man, he is one sick puppy."

But Agent P didn't hear that last part. He had already raced out of his secret lair, knowing that there wasn't a moment to lose if his sworn enemy and nemesis, the evil Dr. Doofenshmirtz, was hatching a new evil plot!

Meanwhile, at Baljeet's house, he, Phineas, and Ferb worked together to build the portal to Mars. The three boys carted massive pipes through the living room and brought over nearly all of Phineas and Ferb's tools. There were large hoops and even larger rings which needed to be welded together. The sound of buzzing power tools and banging hammers blared through the house.

The biggest problem the boys faced was that Baljeet had never really built anything before! He couldn't tell a hammer from a screwdriver, and he didn't even know which end of each tool to use! More than once, Baljeet knocked over boxes full of bolts and nuts, making enormous messes that everyone had to help clean up. Baljeet even got a wrench stuck on his nose! But with a little help from Phineas and Ferb, Baljeet passed his crash course in construction.

Finally, Phineas strapped on a safety harness and hovered above the portal's sophisticated control panel. He carefully programmed the coordinates so that the portal would be able to open a window to Mars . . .

just in case anyone wanted to travel there.

At last, the portal to Mars was ready! The boys stood back to admire their work.

"You're all set for the science fair tomorrow!" Phineas told Baljeet.

Baljeet grinned. He was sure that an A grade would be his . . . all thanks to some help from Phineas and Ferb!

Phineas and Ferb took another good look at the portal. It had three wide steps leading up to a large circular frame. Inside, a glowing

purple light rotated around and around in a circle. There was a red light at the very top of the portal and a large lever on the side for controlling the operation. Their portal to Mars was nothing if not a piece of very sophisticated technology!

But was it good enough to win first place in the science fair? There was only one way to find out!

The next morning, Phineas and Ferb hurried over to the Googolplex Mall, where the science fair would be held later that day. A long row of cubicles had been arranged in the middle of the mall, with a separate one for each science-fair participant. To the boys' surprise, Baljeet's portal to Mars was completely assembled in the small cubicle he had been assigned.

17

"Wow, Baljeet, you're already set up!" Phineas exclaimed.

"I have been here since midnight waiting for everyone," Baljeet replied through clenched teeth. A huge grin was plastered across his face. "I can't stop smiling. I have got cramps in my cheeks."

"Here, let me help you," said Phineas. He grabbed Baljeet's cheeks, stretched them out, and shook them back and forth to loosen up the muscles. "There you go, buddy."

"Ahhh." Baljeet sighed in relief. "Now I will just hang out and be cool until my teacher gets here."

But in seconds, his cheeks froze into an extreme grin once more. "Uh-oh! It is happening again!" Baljeet exclaimed gleefully. This time, there wasn't anything that Phineas or Ferb could do to help him. Until Baljeet's teacher saw the portal to Mars and the judges had examined his work, Baljeet was going to be stuck in a state of barely controlled anticipation!

Across the mall, Phineas and Ferb's older sister, Candace Flynn, was camped out in the food court with a pair of high-powered binoculars. She smiled to herself as she peered through the lenses. Candace would be more than happy to stay there all day watching her adorable crush, Jeremy Johnson, hard at work at Mr. Slushy Dawg.

"Oh, Jeremy," Candace said aloud to

herself. "No one makes a corn dog like you!"

Just then, Jeremy looked directly at her. It turned out that he wasn't all the way across the food court as she had thought. Instead, he was standing right in front of her!

"Oh, hi, Candace," he said, waving two giant corn dogs at her. "Nice binoculars!"

Candace dropped the binoculars and laughed awkwardly. "Yep. Yep, they are *definitely* working," she said quickly, trying to cover up the fact that she'd been staring at Jeremy through them! She walked up to the counter to show the binoculars to Jeremy. "Heh. I just bought these from my dad and was, uh, you know, making sure that they work! And they sure do. You can see really far away or really up close."

Then Candace noticed a small sign. "Help Wanted?" she asked.

"Yeah, you should apply," Jeremy replied. "We could work together."

"You mean side by side?" Candace asked breathlessly. Spending hours every day with Jeremy, working together to make Danville's best burgers and corn dogs? That would be a dream come true!

Suddenly, a girl zipped in front of Jeremy, completely blocking Candace. "Hi there!" she exclaimed. "I'm really, really motivated. Really, really, really positive. Really, really high energy. I would like to apply for the job."

"Excuse me," Candace said, politely moving the girl out of the way. "I—I would also like to apply for the job."

Just then, Jeremy's boss walked over. "Well, ladies, I'm afraid I only have one opening," he said. "How about a competition to see who gets the job?"

"Sounds like a great idea to me," the girl, whose name was Wendy, said as she narrowed her eyes. "Good luck." Then she stuck her hand out to Candace—but whipped it away just as Candace reached out to shake it. "Ooh, too slow! I think I'll call *you* Molasses!"

Then Wendy waved dismissively and walked away.

"Molasses," grumbled Candace. "Well, I think I'll call you something . . . *slower* than molasses. That's for sure."

Suddenly, Candace looked up to see Jeremy and his boss staring at her.

"This isn't part of the competition, is it?" she asked quickly. Because Candace was determined to win . . . and falling behind in the sarcastic nickname category was not going to help her cause!

At the same time, Agent P was zipping through the streets of Danville, using his rocket-powered jetpack to follow a Doofenshmirtz Evil, Incorporated truck at top speed. There was something big and bulky in the back of the truck. It was completely covered by a beige tarp, and Agent P was determined to find out what it was. He maneuvered the jetpack until he was in position to jump onto the truck's bumper. Then, holding on tightly, Agent P shimmied along the side of the truck and leaped in through the passenger window.

Dr. Doofenshmirtz, who was wearing a strange set of overalls with short pants that had an intricate design embroidered on them, was at the wheel. Agent P took one look at the pants and realized that they were the dreaded lederhosen that Major Monogram had warned him about!

"Ooh, Perry the Platypus, welcome to my truck of doom!" Dr. Doofenshmirtz cried when he saw his passenger. The evil doctor pushed a button and before Agent P could jump out of the way, he found himself strapped into a baby's car seat, with a mobile dangling over his head!

"I suppose you're wondering why I'm wearing lederhosen," Dr. Doofenshmirtz continued, gesturing to his bizarre outfit as he slammed on the brakes. He thrust a bony leg onto the steering wheel. "What? I've got the legs for it! Anyway, it will all become clear soon enough."

The screech of brakes blasted through the air as a truck pulled up behind them. "Come on, Hansel! Move it!" a gruff voice shouted.

Dr. Doofenshmirtz blasted his horn. "Hey, wise guy! I'm expl— Oh! Oh-ho-ho! Sorry, *madam*! Sorry." Dr. Doofenshmirtz chuckled as he glanced back and realized that the person in the truck behind him was actually a woman! He leaned closer to Agent P and continued, "The voice was so masculine and growly, I thought it must be a man's. I mean, people must call her 'sir' all the time on the phone. It must be so em—"

Dr. Doofenshmirtz grew pale as he noticed an odd look on Agent P's face. "She's standing right behind me now, isn't she?"

He tried to roll up the window, but it was too late.

Thwack!

A thick fist flew through the window and popped the evil doctor right in the face! In an instant, a purple-and-blue bruise started to bloom around his swollen eye. "Not one word, Perry the Platypus," he ordered.

Dr. Doofenshmirtz didn't say anything else as he pulled up at the Googolplex Mall. He shoved the car seat—with Agent P still in it—into a wagon and hitched up whatever was beneath the tarp. Then he pulled everything toward the science fair registration desk. A line of kids stretched down the hallway and through the mall, almost reaching the doors.

"Oh, great, a line," Dr. Doofenshmirtz grumbled. Then he sneered at the scrawny kid standing in front of him. "What is this, a model of Pluto?" he asked sarcastically. "That planet doesn't even exist anymore, you moron!"

As Dr. Doofenshmirtz laughed rudely, a big, brawny guy walked up to them. "Thanks for holding my spot in line, little brother," he said as he reached for the model of Pluto. Then he turned to Dr. Doofenshmirtz. "What were you saying about Pluto?"

"Nothing," Dr. Doofenshmirtz replied quickly, holding up his hands. "I'm sure it's a—"

Thwack!

Now Dr. Doofenshmirtz had *two* black eyes—*and* a model of Pluto stuck on his head!

"I suppose you're wondering why I'm putting myself through all of this," Dr. Doofenshmirtz said with a sigh to Agent P, who was still trapped in the car seat. The evil scientist closed his eyes as he drifted back to memories of his youth in Gimmelshtoomp.

"When I was young, I entered a science fair with my very first '-inator,'" Dr. Doofenshmirtz recalled. "I was—I wasn't very clever with names yet. It was just, you know, -inator."

Even though it had been many years, Dr. Doofenshmirtz could still clearly remember his very first invention. It was made up of an enormous metal cylinder with all sorts

of strange fins and discs protruding from it. And best of all, his -inator was the color of creamed spinach from a can.

"Just as I was about to demonstrate my invention to the judges, a kid with a baking-soda volcano stole the show," Dr. Doofenshmirtz continued bitterly. So many years had passed, and he *still* couldn't believe the judges had been so wowed by mixing vinegar and baking soda to simulate a frothy, foamy volcano eruption. Sure, it was kind of cool—but was it first-prize-science-fair-winning cool? Dr. Doofenshmirtz hardly thought so!

"The next year I tried again with my Even Bigger-inator. And again, my thunder was stolen by a baking-soda volcano! I'd had enough of science. I decided to devote my life to poetry instead," the evil doctor continued.

Dr. Doofenshmirtz recited one of his very own original poems, just as he had in a hip, artsy café back in Gimmelshtoomp:

"The movies are gray.
The TV is black.
The horses are running.
Please bring me some food.

"Yet curiously, I *still* lost to a baking-soda volcano!" Dr. Doofenshmirtz cried. "But never again!"

With a dramatic flourish, Dr. Doofenshmirtz ripped off the beige tarp. "Behold, the World's Largest Baking-Soda Volcano!" he announced grandly.

At last, Agent P could see what had been hidden beneath the tarp: an enormous model of a volcano!

"I mean, it—it has to be the biggest one here, right?" Dr. Doofenshmirtz continued. "It's got to win. I feel confident."

"Next!" a voice called out.

"Ooh, we're next!" Dr. Doofenshmirtz cried giddily. He hurried over to the check-in desk, pulling the wagon with Agent P behind him.

The man at the desk raised his eyebrows as Dr. Doofenshmirtz approached. "Aren't you a little old to be entering this science fair?"

"No, what makes you say that?" Dr. Doofenshmirtz asked loudly. "I—I mean, look at me. I'm wearing lederhosen."

"Okay . . . go ahead," the man replied.

"Heh-heh. See? I know what I'm doing," Dr. Doofenshmirtz whispered to Agent P.

Agent P wasn't so sure, though. He'd witnessed a lot of Dr. Doofenshmirtz's half-baked plots . . . and they tended to backfire worse than anyone could possibly imagine!

But who knows? Maybe this time Dr. Doofenshmirtz would be successful!

Chapter
THREE

"Hi, Mr. McGillicuddy!" Baljeet's voice rang out happily. It was the moment he'd been waiting for—his science teacher had just arrived to judge his project. Baljeet could practically taste the A he was sure he would receive.

"Well, I see you've built yourself a proto-type," Mr. McGillicuddy began, "but the question still remains . . . does . . . it . . . work?"

"Well, I think—" Baljeet started to say.

But Phineas cut him off. "Of course it works! Fire it up!"

Phineas, Ferb, and Baljeet put on sunglasses to protect their eyes. Then Baljeet pulled the lever. The center of the portal blazed with a rotating purple light; even Mr. McGillicuddy had to shield his eyes from its intense shine.

A few seconds later, the center of the portal revealed a scene that was oddly familiar: dozens of identical gray cubicles, each one featuring a science project and an excited participant.

"Okay, so I see the science fair," the teacher commented.

"Take a closer look, Mr. McGillicuddy," Baljeet encouraged him.

When Mr. McGillicuddy leaned into the portal, what he saw was astonishing! "Wow, a science fair on Mars!" he gasped as he watched small, lime-green aliens zip around the cubicles. The aliens each had three eyes, strange ears sticking out from the sides of their faces, and knobby antennae on the tops of their heads.

"Baljeet, you have just validated my entire career as an educator!" Mr. McGillicuddy continued breathlessly. "You get an A-plus-plus-plus! I'm going to go get the judges!"

Just a few cubicles away, Dr. Doofenshmirtz was putting the finishing touches on his volcano model. "Soon, I will show them the havoc created when an acid and a base combine!" He cackled gleefully. "But first, I have to find an outlet, 'cause there's a nice little laser show that goes along with it."

Dr. Doofenshmirtz walked a few steps until he found the nearest electrical outlet. There was only one problem—it already had a cord plugged into it. "All right, we'll just take this out and put mine in," he said.

At that moment, Mr. McGillicuddy brought the three science-fair judges over to Baljeet's portal to Mars. "It's right over here," the teacher said to them. "Baljeet, show our judges what Mr. McGillicuddy has taught you!"

Once more, Baljeet pulled the lever.

But this time, nothing happened!

A look of panic crossed Mr. McGillicuddy's face. He rushed over to the lever and started pushing it back and forth, but still, nothing happened! Baljeet and Phineas exchanged a worried glance. What they didn't know was that Dr. Doofenshmirtz had just unplugged Baljeet's project. Without electricity to power the portal, it wouldn't work at all!

"Ah, um, eh, uh—just a moment," Mr. McGillicuddy stammered, slamming the lever back and forth. "It takes the skilled hand of a master professor!" Then he jumped right in front of the portal and started waving his arms. "Hello? Mr. Martian? It's Mr. McGillicuddy!"

The science teacher turned back to the judges and giggled nervously. "*Uno momento!*" he cried before he rushed off to find out what was wrong with the portal.

"Who's up for corn dogs?" one of the judges asked.

"I am!" another judge replied.

Mr. McGillicuddy was so eager to fix the portal that he didn't even notice that the judges had wandered off to the food court. "Aha!" he exclaimed when he found a control panel on the back of the portal with the dial set to low. "Turn it all the way up to high. Yes! That should do it!"

He rushed back to the lever and yanked it again, but the portal still didn't turn on—because it still wasn't plugged in.

"I wonder what's wrong with the portal," Phineas said thoughtfully.

"Oh, no matter," Baljeet replied. "Personally, I never cared about winning. I just wanted a good grade!"

Phineas shrugged. "Well, who's up for corn dogs?" he asked.

"Me!" cried Baljeet.

Phineas, Ferb, and Baljeet set off for the Mr. Slushy Dawg in the food court—but they had no idea what was happening behind the counter. In the kitchen, Candace and Wendy were about to embark on the hot-dog battle of the century!

The manager set a tray of hot dogs in front of each of them. "Girls, your first task is to dress these dogs with ketchup and mustard," he explained. "I'll be back in a little bit to check your work. Good luck!"

As soon as the manager left, Candace and Wendy squared off like a pair of cowboys in a Western showdown. They spent only a moment glaring at each other before each girl grabbed a bottle of ketchup and a bottle of mustard—one in each hand—and started squirting the hot dogs furiously!

Bright red-and-yellow squiggles coated each hot dog, until suddenly, Candace's ketchup bottle jammed. "No fair!" she cried, shaking the bottle wildly. "I ran out of ketchup!"

Splurt!

A huge glob of ketchup squirted out of the bottle—and landed right on top of Wendy's head!

"Oops," Candace said sheepishly. "*Now* I'm out of ketchup!"

Wendy's eyes narrowed as she realized what Candace had done. She carefully aimed her bottle of mustard at Candace and squeezed it with all her strength.

Splat!

A massive glob of mustard flew out of the bottle and splashed all over Candace's face, making a mustard beard that dripped down her chin.

"Oops," Wendy said smugly. "Now *I'm* out of mustard!"

Candace didn't stop to think. She grabbed a bright green bottle and squirted it at Wendy.

Sploosh!

"Oh, look," Candace said, gritting her teeth. "I'm out of relish!"

The green condiment sprayed all over Wendy's eyes, until it looked as if she was wearing a pair of goggles made of chopped-up pickles! To retaliate, Wendy threw a squeeze tube of mayonnaise on the counter. Then she slammed it with a heavy metal tray.

Splash!

Now Candace was covered from head to toe in ooey, gooey, drippy, sticky mayonnaise!

She didn't even bother to wipe the mayonnaise out of her eyes before she threw a handful of pickles right at Wendy's face.

The food fight was on.

And Candace was ready to take it to the next level!

Back at the science fair, Mr. McGillicuddy was desperate. He'd tried everything—or *almost* everything—but the portal to Mars still wasn't working!

"It has to work! It has to work!" he repeated again and again, yanking the lever so hard that he lost his balance and fell backward. But his clumsiness turned out to be a stroke of good luck for the science teacher; from the floor, he noticed the long power cord stretching from the portal. Right away, he decided to follow it.

As Mr. McGillicuddy crawled along the floor next to the cord, Agent P yanked himself out of the bottom half of his custom-made platypus suit. Sure, it was humiliating to walk around the science fair in his underwear, but he *had* to get out of that car seat so that he could stop Dr. Doofenshmirtz's latest plot! With a quick click of a button on his remote control, Agent P locked his platypus bottoms in the seat and zoomed off in his polka-dot underwear.

Dr. Doofenshmirtz stood on a tall railing above his model volcano, holding a gigantic

jar of vinegar that was bigger than he was. He carefully positioned it over the mouth of the volcano. "Now just add some vinegar and . . ." he said—right before Agent P landed on his head! "Ahhhhh!"

At the same moment, Mr. McGillicuddy reached the electrical outlet. "It just wasn't plugged in!" he exclaimed. But instead of unplugging Dr. Doofenshmirtz's project, Mr. McGillicuddy's eyes landed on another electrical outlet nearby—one that was labeled HIGH VOLTAGE. He laughed eagerly at the thought of loading up the portal with even more power than before!

Then Mr. McGillicuddy raced back to the portal and pulled the lever. At once, the whirling purple light filled its entryway. "It's working! It's working!" he cried in delight.

"Ew, gross! I smell like salad!" Dr. Doofenshmirtz complained as he sloshed around in an enormous puddle of vinegar. He tried to stand up, but his feet slipped on the slick tiles. Suddenly, he pitched over the railing and landed in the mouth of his model volcano! As vinegar dripped off his clothes into the powdery mound of baking soda hidden inside the volcano, Dr. Doofenshmirtz knew that a chemical reaction was starting that nobody, not even an evil scientist such as himself, could stop.

"Say good-bye to this pair of lederhosen," he said aloud to himself as the volcano began to tremble and quake. Agent P raced off

to safety as Dr. Doofenshmirtz's experiment exploded—sending the evil doctor, along with tiny pieces of his model volcano, into the air!

At that very moment, Baljeet's portal to Mars, juiced up with way too much power, went into overdrive! It emitted a bright beam that blasted through the Googolplex Mall, capturing Dr. Doofenshmirtz and all the pieces of his erupted volcano in its eerie purple light. Instead of plunging to the floor, everything bobbed in the air, free from the force of gravity.

"Hey, I'm unhurt!" Dr. Doofenshmirtz exclaimed. "Yes! I am invincible!"

Then the portal began to suck in the purple beam—and everything floating inside it.

"Wait-wait-wait! Where are we going?" Dr. Doofenshmirtz asked.

Zzzzzzzzzap!

Suddenly, the portal swallowed the beam, the volcano pieces, Dr. Doofenshmirtz—and even itself! Mr. McGillicuddy was left alone in the cubicle, blinking in disbelief.

Then the three judges walked up to him, munching on their corn dogs. "All right, so what was it you wanted to show us?" one of them asked.

"N-n-n-no! It-it *was* here!" Mr. McGillicuddy stammered in shock. "Ah, uh—"

"Come on," one judge said to the others. "Let's go find a *real* winner."

And off they went, still eating their corn dogs, leaving Mr. McGillicuddy alone in the cubicle, babbling to himself in shock.

"Excuse me!" a little girl called out as she approached the judges. She was wearing a special backpack that had four long robotic arms sticking out of it. Each of her hands held a control stick. "Am I too late to enter?"

"Are those mechanical arms?" one of the judges asked.

"Why, yes," the girl replied. "I used them to make this baking-soda volcano!"

She gestured to a small red wagon next to her. It was carrying a model volcano that looked just like Dr. Doofenshmirtz's—except it was only a fraction of the size.

"A baking-soda volcano?" gasped a judge. "Cool! First prize!"

From Baljeet's cubicle, a tiny cloud of purple light appeared right next to the still-stammering Mr. McGillicuddy.

"Oh, come on!" Dr. Doofenshmirtz's voice echoed through the light.

But all Mr. McGillicuddy could do was stand there and stammer!

Back at the food court, the manager of Mr. Slushy Dawg didn't realize what Candace and Wendy were doing until it was too late—*way* too late. The kitchen was a disaster, with gloppy puddles of condiments on the food trays, the counters, and even the floor. But compared to the two girls, the kitchen looked great. Candace and Wendy were covered in so much ketchup, mustard, mayonnaise, and

relish that they looked like a pair of condiment monsters!

"Well, seeing as how you've used most of

my ketchup and mustard to dress yourselves, I'm afraid *neither* of you get the job," the manager told them.

"Snail!" Candace suddenly exclaimed, pointing at Wendy as she thought of the perfect insult for the girl who'd nicknamed her Molasses. "I'll call you Snail! Ha!"

"Ooh, you're quick," Wendy shot back sarcastically.

Far from the chaos at the food court and the science fair, Baljeet, Phineas, Ferb, and Isabella snagged a bench where they could enjoy their corn dogs in peace.

"I just can't believe you guys built a portal to Mars and didn't go through it yourselves!" Isabella marveled.

Phineas and Ferb exchanged a grin. "Oh, we did!" Phineas replied.

"But that's another story," Ferb added. And it was one that he and his brother would never forget.

Just then, Phineas spotted his pet platypus. "Oh, look. There's Perry!" Phineas exclaimed. His platypus always seemed to be wandering off somewhere. But he always made it back home eventually!

It all started the day before, while Phineas and Ferb were helping Baljeet build his portal to Mars. Back at home, Candace had a difficult decision to make. She sprawled across the bed in her pink-and-purple room as she fiddled with her cell phone. "Let's see," she said aloud thoughtfully, "who should I call first to hang out with? How 'bout Jeremy?"

She speed-dialed him—of course Candace

had her crush on speed dial!—and waited for Jeremy to answer his phone.

"Hey, it's Jeremy," his voice sounded in her ear. "You know what to do after the . . ."

Candace frowned when Jeremy's voice mail picked up. It was hard enough to find the courage to call him. Leaving a message was next to impossible! "Uh, hey, Jeremy. It's Candace," she began. "Just seeing what's going on today. Call me back if you want to. Okay. Bye."

As Candace hung up, she sighed. "Aw, man. That never gets easier. Oh well. I'll just call Stacy. She's probably been waiting by the phone all morning."

While she waited for Stacy to answer her phone, Candace grinned. Hanging out with her best friend in the whole world was always a great way to spend the day!

But Stacy's voice mail immediately came on, before her phone even had a chance to ring. "You've reached Stacy's mobile. Leave a message and I'll get back to you."

"Hey, Stace. It's Candace. Where are you? Call me!"

"Hmm, that's weird," Candace said after she hung up. "Who else can I call? I know! Jenny! I haven't seen her since the boys built a beach in the backyard!"

Candace quickly dialed Jenny and crossed her fingers, hoping that she would answer.

"Hello?"

"Uh, Jenny! Hey, it's Candy!" Candace exclaimed.

"Leave me a message and I'll get back to you as soon as possible," Jenny's voice continued. So Jenny *hadn't* answered the phone—it was just her voice mail, too!

"Call me!" Candace chirped into the phone. Then she started racking her brain for other people who might want to hang out. "Hmm, who else do I know?"

Candace started calling just about every single person she'd ever met in her life . . . and leaving a message for each one.

"Becky, this is Candace. I know we haven't talked since kindergarten, but—

"Hey, Wendy. This is Candace. Uh, we shared a seat on the bus to the planetarium—

"Hello, Clarissa? This is Candace. We played volleyball at camp."

Candace called Jill. She called Nancy. She called Barbara and Olga and Joe. Finally, out of sheer desperation, she called Information.

"Information," the operator said.

"See a movie with me!" Candace demanded. Then she screamed in frustration. "Where *is* everyone? Are they all out having fun without me?"

Candace was so lost in thought that she never even noticed Perry sneaking off through a filing cabinet to a top secret briefing from Major Monogram about Dr. Doofenshmirtz's recent lederhosen purchase.

"So all my friends need some time to themselves, huh?" Candace asked, narrowing her eyes. "Well, not without me, they don't!" She jammed a helmet on her head and ran down to the garage, where she jumped on her bike and pedaled furiously toward the Googolplex Mall.

Her first stop was Mr. Slushy Dawg, where Jeremy worked. But his boss hadn't seen him all day. "Yeah, I'm looking for Jeremy, too," he said. "I need him to work tomorrow. Our fry guy just defected over to Taco Tepee."

Across the food court, the owner of the Taco Tepee smiled smugly from under his sombrero. For good measure, he put an arm around his newest employee—just to rub it in. Candace glanced at the Taco Tepee out of the corner of her eye and decided to keep quiet. She had no interest in getting in the middle of this feud!

"Am I *that* bad to hang out with?" Candace asked herself as she headed home. She was so bummed out that

she didn't even have the energy to ride her bike anymore. Instead, she just sadly pushed it along the sidewalk.

Suddenly, her phone beeped. Candace's heart soared. Someone was trying to get in touch with her!

"Ooh, a text message! And it's from Stacy!" she squealed in excitement. Then Candace read the message aloud. "C-Y-L-B-F-F-S."

A look of confusion crossed Candace's face. "What does that mean?" she wondered as she tried to figure out the cryptic message. "Let's see . . . 'Candace you loser, bad friend-ships fail, Stacy.' Harsh!"

Candace wandered over to a birdbath—but one look at her sad face made the pigeons in it fly away. "It feels like I don't exist any-more," she said, staring at her reflection in the rippling water. "Like I'm a nobody. I wish I could go to some cool, faraway place and start over."

Then Candace noticed something nearby. "Wait a minute! Those are Phineas's and Ferb's bikes!" she exclaimed. Her wandering had landed her right in front of Baljeet's house.

Inside, the boys had just finished building the portal to Mars, and they were taking a moment to watch the purple light whirling inside the entrance before Phineas and Ferb went back home. "Inside, I am thanking you a thousand times," Baljeet told Phineas and Ferb.

"See you tomorrow!" Phineas called out just as Candace charged into the room.

"What are you guys up to?" she demanded. If she couldn't hang out with any of her friends, busting her brothers would have to do!

"We just built a teleport to a cool, faraway place," Phineas explained.

Candace's eyes lit up. "Well, that's all I

needed to hear!" she exclaimed. "Candace Flynn is out. Peace!"

Candace skipped up the stairs of the portal and walked right through the entrance, onto rust-colored dirt under a shimmery magenta sky.

"Welcome to Mars!" Phineas announced.

Candace spun around in horror. *"Mars?!"*

Zzzzzap! Without warning, the interior of the portal started to sizzle and crackle, flashing blinding lights throughout Baljeet's bedroom.

Suddenly it disappeared in a cloud of black smoke, leaving only the portal's exterior! Even worse—Candace disappeared with it!

"The portal is broken!" howled Baljeet. "Oh, now I will not get a good grade at the science fair tomorrow . . . and there's also the issue of your sister stranded on a distant, barren planet."

"Don't worry, we can fix it," Phineas said confidently. "Candace is probably laughing about it as we speak!"

Alone on the red planet, Candace wasn't laughing. Instead, she was angrily yelling—"PHINEAS!"

Across town at the headquarters of Doofenshmirtz Evil, Incorporated, Agent P cut through the wall with a laser. Then he burst in, ready to use the element of surprise to get the upper hand on Dr. Doofenshmirtz!

"Perry the Platypus?" Dr. Doofenshmirtz asked, barely looking up from the plans he was working on. "Oh, are you here to—oh, no, no, no. I—I'm running a little behind. I'm still in the middle of basic plotting and scheming. Plus, I can't give you my evil-scheme monologue because I write that last. Sorry, that's just how I roll."

Agent P turned away and walked over to the hole he'd made in the wall, fully intending to come back later to foil Dr. Doofenshmirtz.

Just then, the evil scientist had an idea. "Wait! Wait! Wait! Why don't you help me? That way I can finish faster and you can defeat me faster! It's . . . it's win-win! Let me grab my coupons. We'll start by shopping for some supplies."

Agent P was skeptical. This was a very unusual approach to fighting evil. But just because something was unusual didn't mean it wouldn't work. And he was willing to do anything to sabotage Dr. Doofenshmirtz's latest plot.

Even if it meant having to go on a shopping spree with him!

Chapter
FIVE

Many millions of miles away, Candace yelled as loudly as she could, "You guys are so busted!"

But the only sound in response was her own voice, echoing off the dusty plains and barren red-rock mountains of Mars.

Now I truly am alone, Candace realized quietly. But before she could start feeling too scared, a robotic vehicle equipped with a camera and solar panels rolled by her.

"Hey, it's one of those Mars rovers!" Candace exclaimed gleefully. "I'm saved!"

At NASA headquarters back on Earth, an exhausted scientist with bloodshot eyes stared and stared at the enormous panoramic screen in front of him. It was his job to sit there, keeping an eye out for signs of life on Mars. There was only one problem, though: the display never changed! All he saw were red rocks, more red rocks, and even more red rocks. Finally, he could no longer bear another minute of staring.

"Ahhhhh!" he screamed, leaping out of his chair and turning his back on the display screen. "I can't take it anymore! I've been staring at red rocks for twenty years! That's all there are on that stupid planet—red rocks! Face it, there's no life on Mars! That's it! I'm shutting this place down. Game over!"

All through his loud tantrum, the scientist

never once turned around to peek at the monitor. If he had, he would have been surprised—no, *shocked*—to see Candace Flynn waving her arms, frantically trying to get someone's attention!

The scientist slammed his fist on a button, and the screen went dark just as Candace was trying to juggle Mars rocks in front of the camera. On the red planet, the rover suddenly shut down, folding up before her eyes.

"Stupid rover!" Candace yelled in frustration as she started kicking it. "You're not going to ignore me, too! Take that you ugly, unmanned, exploratory vehicle! And that! Yeah! Yeah, that's what I thought!"

Candace's attack on the rover made so much noise that a little green head with three stacked eyes and a round-tipped antenna popped up from behind a rock.

It was a real Martian!

The Martian scurried over to Candace as she stood in triumph over the heap of smoldering wreckage that once was the Mars rover. Cautiously, the Martian poked at the rover, then cringed. It was clear to Candace that the Martian was afraid of the robotic rover.

"Huh?" Candace asked in shock. "What *are* you?"

"Luis!" the Martian yelled. Suddenly, from behind nearly every rock, hillside, and mountain, dozens of Martians appeared. They came running, chattering, and making all sorts of noises that Candace couldn't understand.

One of the Martians made an odd sound and pointed at Candace. All the other Martians immediately surrounded her and lifted her high into the air.

"What's going on? What are you doing? Put me down!" Candace yelled.

But the Martians didn't listen to her demands. Instead, they just carried her off across the dusty red plains. There was nothing Candace could do to get away!

At Baljeet's house, Phineas, Ferb, and Baljeet had been working hard to get the portal to Mars functioning again.

"There! I think we've fixed it!" Phineas exclaimed. At last, the entrance orb was glowing with that revolving purple light. As the light vanished, a golden-brown planet with a swirly yellow sky appeared in the portal's entrance.

"No, that is Venus," Baljeet pointed out.

Phineas carefully adjusted one of the dials, and a ferocious dinosaur appeared in a wild landscape of tall palm trees and smoking volcanoes.

"And *that* is Earth in prehistoric times," Baljeet said.

Suddenly, the dinosaur charged right at them!

"Ahhh! Ahhh!" Baljeet cried. "Change it! Change it! Change it!"

Phineas spun the dial again, and the portal displayed a curious sight: Baljeet, Phineas, and Ferb standing at a portal that displayed an image of Mars.

"Whoo! Hey, look! It is us in the future, fixing the portal!" Baljeet exclaimed.

From inside the portal, the other Baljeet waved and said, "Hello, Baljeet of the past.

Just watch us. That is how we learned to fix it. Gesundheit!"

"Thanks," Baljeet replied to himself—right before he sneezed.

The boys watched their future selves demonstrate how to repair the portal. Then Phineas and Ferb started tinkering with the portal in real time. Moments later, their portal opened a window to Mars! The boys' repair efforts had finally paid off!

"It worked! Cool!" Phineas cheered as he and Ferb walked through the portal. He turned back to Baljeet, who was staying behind. "Okay, give us twenty minutes to find Candace, then open up the portal."

"Oh, please be careful!" Baljeet cried, wringing his hands nervously. "I still need your help at the science fair tomorrow!"

Zzzap! The portal snapped shut before Baljeet could say another word.

Phineas and Ferb took a minute to look around the red planet. "Hmm . . ." Phineas said as he noticed the battered Mars rover that Candace had destroyed. "Something tells me that Candace was here. Good thing you brought your tools. I have an idea!"

Meanwhile, the cluster of Martians carried Candace past the rust-colored mountains to a secret place filled with bubbling pools of lava and a strange, castlelike structure made out of maroon-colored bricks. It had tall, open arches all around it. Inside the space castle, the Martians brought Candace over to a gleaming golden throne. To Candace's surprise, they plunked her right down on its plush seat!

"Okay, what's going on?" Candace asked.

When one of the Martians placed a glittery crown on her head, Candace started to understand everything. "Ohhh, you're making me your ruler!" she exclaimed.

The Martians cheered in response. Then they pulled up a long banquet table filled with Martian delicacies.

"Cool! Let's get this party started!" commanded Candace. "Crank the tunes!"

The Martians just looked at her in confusion, blinking their many wide eyes.

"Uh, you know, *music*?" Candace tried to explain. But still the Martians stared at her blankly. "You guys don't know what music is? Well, it's like . . . it's like this."

She grabbed the antenna of the Martian closest to her and pulled it taut. Then Candace began strumming the antenna like it was a guitar, rocking a cool bass riff! All around her, the Martians started bopping up and down in time to the music. They were starting to dance!

"That's it! You're getting it!" Candace cried.

One by one, the other Martians started making music, too. They played their teeth like the keys of a piano and pounded their feet like bongo drums. Some Martians blew on their ears as if they were trumpets, and others dinged their antennas as if they were triangles! Soon her Martian followers had turned into the universe's best backup band, and there was such a rocking song playing that Candace just had to sing.

After all, why shouldn't she celebrate? Everywhere she went, Martians were either hard at work constructing enormous statues of her or following her around to meet her every need. Even from far-off in space, an enormous

model of Candace was now visible on the surface of Mars! There was only one thing that could ruin the best afternoon of Candace's life. . . .

"Follow that music, Ferb!" Phineas yelled as the brothers zoomed off in the rover they had just repaired.

"You are much more attentive than my friends on Earth," Candace said to the crowd of tiny Martians around her. "And better at building statues of me! Come on, let's walk and talk! Of course, I'll do most of the talking. To make things easier, I'll call you 'good Stacy' and you 'good Jenny' and . . . huh?"

Candace looked confused as another cluster of Martians approached her, carrying a Mars rover. They started babbling at her in their language, so at first she didn't realize what they were saying.

In a flash of understanding, everything became clear to her, and Candace knew *exactly* what the Martians wanted. "Oh, okay," she said indulgently. "What the heck!"

Candace lifted up her foot and stomped on the rover until it crumpled. Then all the Martians cheered for their queen!

Suddenly, a familiar voice rose above all the rest. "Hey, Candace!"

"Phineas? Ferb?" Candace asked in surprise, spinning around to look for her brothers.

"We're here to rescue you!" Phineas announced as their rover rolled up to Candace and the Martians.

"Why would I go back to being a nobody when I can be the queen of *here*?" Candace replied.

A crew of Martians hurried over to the boys' rover and started pounding on it with their little fists.

"Well, there's a lot of . . . uh, Candace? What's up with your friends?" Phineas asked.

"Ah, ignore them," she said with a wave of her hand. "They're harmless. Hey! Why don't you hang out a while so you can tell everyone how popular I've become?"

Candace grinned at Phineas and Ferb as she imagined them back on Earth, spreading the word about her golden crown, her adoring fans, and her very own planet to rule as she wished. Becoming the queen of Mars was about a thousand times cooler than hanging out at the mall . . . and it would be even cooler when all her Earth friends found out about it!

Back on Earth, Agent P and the evil Dr. Doofenshmirtz arrived at an enormous megamart—the kind of store stocked with just about anything anyone could ever need. As Agent P perched in the kiddie seat of a metal shopping cart, Dr. Doofenshmirtz consulted his list. "Okay, I've already got the chicken wire," he reported. "Let's see . . . oh, here. You take the list and cross things off as we go. Should we get something for later, like a—like one of those big pickles or a three-bean salad?"

WHAM!

As the shopping cart crashed into something, Dr. Doofenshmirtz and Agent P looked up from their list . . . just in time to find themselves face-to-face with Major Monogram and his assistant, Carl Karl! The greatest threat to the Tri-State Area and the man dedicated to stopping his evil plots were staring at each other right in front of a display of hair dryers. Just like Dr. Doofenshmirtz, Major Monogram was pushing a cart. And just like Agent P, Carl was riding in it!

Major Monogram and Carl said nothing—not a single word—as Major Monogram began slowly walking backward, dragging the cart with him, and looking anywhere *except* at Dr. Doofenshmirtz and Agent P!

That's when Major Monogram and Agent P

both realized that the best way to handle this unbelievably weird situation was to just pretend that it had never happened.

"Well," Dr. Doofenshmirtz said in a low voice, "that was awkward."

And that, Agent P thought, was the understatement of the year!

Far away on Mars, Candace sprawled across her golden throne, staring into space with a bored look on her face. Not even the crowd of gibbering Martians at her feet, shaking a miniature Martian doll and making Martian music, could entertain her. No, what Candace *really* wanted right now was a little time by herself—without dozens of adoring subjects waiting to dote on her!

"Uh, I'm just going to go for a walk," Candace said as she scrambled down from her throne. But she'd hardly gone five steps before another posse of Martians approached, dragging a rover that they wanted her to smash.

"Uh, guys? Not now, okay?" she said, trying to be polite. "No, really."

But then another group of Martians hurried up to her, and another, and another. Before she knew it, she was completely surrounded!

"I would just like to go for a walk alone!" she insisted.

Luckily for Candace, the sound of screeching brakes suddenly echoed through the space castle. "There you are!" she yelled as Phineas and Ferb rolled up in their rover. Candace was hardly able to hide her relief. "Where have you guys been?"

"Ferb was just explaining to the Martians how we got here," replied Phineas.

"Oh," Candace said. Then Phineas's words sunk in. "Wait, *what*?"

"Ferb speaks Martian," Phineas said. "They're really excited about the idea of a science fair."

Candace looked around and saw dozens of Martians building cubicles for their science fair and decorating them with colorful banners. "Figures. I'm the queen of little green nerds," Candace grumbled. "Can you tell them that I just want a little time to myself?"

Ferb opened his mouth and said something in Martian language. After one of them quickly responded, Ferb turned back to Candace. "They say 'Fine, but not without them,'" Ferb translated for her.

"Argh!" Candace yelled in frustration. Then she took a deep breath and tried to explain things calmly. "Okay, but just because I need to do things without you sometimes doesn't mean I don't like you or appreciate your friendship," she said.

"But Candace, isn't that—" Phineas began.

"Yeah, yeah. Just like my friends with me. Whoop-dee-do!" Candace replied.

Suddenly, the large group of Martians surrounded Phineas and Ferb. The only thing

scarier than the ugly scowls on their faces were their really scary ferocious growls!

"It appears the Martians are blaming us for their queen wanting to leave," Phineas reported.

"Quick, get in!" Candace hollered as she leaped into the rover. As soon as the boys were inside the vehicle, she turned back to the Martians and announced, "Queen Candace is out. Peace!"

Then she blew them a kiss, fired up the rover, and roared away over the red sands.

But the Martians weren't going to give up their queen without a fight! They started screeching in alarm, and then they all tackled one another until they turned into one single, enormous Martian that towered above even the tallest mountain!

"Did you know they could do that?" Phineas asked Candace as they sped away from the mega-Martian.

"No, but get this," Candace said in a gossipy voice. "Every part of their body is a musical instrument, and they never even discovered music before! Martians are so lame!"

She stepped on the gas to make the rover zoom even faster as the mega-Martian started stomping after them.

"Hey Candace, you got your cell phone on you?" asked Phineas. He grabbed the phone and made a fast call. "Hello? Baljeet?"

"How is it we have bars here?" Candace asked in amazement.

"We kind of need you to open the portal now," Phineas continued into the phone.

"They're gaining on us!" shrieked Candace.

The rover raced on, faster than ever, just as the mega-Martian leaped forward in a

last-ditch effort to keep Candace on Mars. Without warning, a shimmery portal opened in front of the rover, and Candace drove right through it and into Baljeet's bedroom! Just as the mega-Martian was about to dive through the portal, it closed as suddenly and unexpectedly as it had opened!

Splat!

The mega-Martian landed face-first on the dry and dusty dirt, left to wonder where it's wonderful queen had gone . . . and why she had taken that miserable rover and those pesky boys with her!

As Dr. Doofenshmirtz and Agent P lugged heavy shopping bags into the headquarters of Doofenshmirtz Evil, Incorporated, the evil scientist turned to the secret agent and smiled. "Perry the Platypus, thanks for your help. I usually hate shopping, but, you know, you make it fun!"

Agent P narrowed his eyes as he spotted something strange on the patio: a bulky hulk of metal that had silvery fins and green discs, and a round ball on the end of a laser beam. He pointed at it and waited for Dr. Doofenshmirtz to tell him what it was.

"What, that?" Dr. Doofenshmirtz asked. "Oh, that's my very first -inator. Good story! I'll tell you all about it tomorrow. Well, I should probably get back to my latest evil scheme. So long . . . sucker!"

Then Dr. Doofenshmirtz stretched out his long legs and kicked the door closed—right in Agent P's face!

Across town, Candace zoomed home from Baljeet's house on her bicycle. When she got there, she started yelling, "Mom! Mom!" as loudly and frantically as she could.

"Well, hello, Candace," her mom said from the backyard. "Where have you been? I want you to see my telescope."

"A telescope?" Candace cried. "Perfect!"

She couldn't wait to tell her mom that she had been the queen of Mars . . . and she knew she could prove it by showing her some of the enormous statues that the Martians had built in her honor.

"Phineas and Ferb built this portal to Mars, and I went through it and was crowned queen of the Martians," Candace said quickly. "Now, I know it sounds crazy, but this time I have proof!"

Candace aimed the telescope at Mars and

adjusted the focus until, at last, the largest Candace statue was easy to see. "What does that look like?" she asked proudly.

But while Candace's mom walked over to the telescope, Dr. Doofenshmirtz examined his very first -inator. "You know, I don't even remember what this does," he said thoughtfully as he started fiddling with some of the buttons. *Whooosh!* When he activated the -inator, a neon-green laser beam jetted off into outer space.

"Oh, that's right," Dr. Doofenshmirtz said, sounding a little disappointed. "It just shoots a beam into space. No wonder I lost to a baking-soda volcano."

As Candace's mom leaned down to peer through the eyepiece, the beam from Dr. Doofenshmirtz's -inator smashed into Mars and completely obliterated the enormous sculpture of Candace's face!

"Hmm . . . well . . . it looks a little like a

monkey wearing a powdered wig," her mom said.

"What? Let me see that!" Candace demanded. Sure enough, when she looked through the telescope, all she could see was the bumpy, rocky surface of Mars. There was no sign of Candace's face anywhere! "B-b-b-bu—" Candace stammered. Then she sighed in defeat.

What else could she do?

Candace walked around to the front yard,

where she sat down in the grass by herself. She held her silent cell phone in her hand and stared at it. No missed calls. No missed texts.

Nobody had been trying to reach her.

"Hey, Candace!" a voice called out.

Candace looked up and saw Jenny, Jeremy, and Stacy approaching her house! She gasped in surprise. "Oh, there you are, guys. Where have you been all day?"

"I was at the dentist," Jenny replied.

"I was taking my little sister to the movies," Jeremy said.

"Didn't you get my text message?" asked Stacy. "'Call You Later. Best Friends Forever? Stacy.'"

"Oh," Candace said, giggling as she remembered what she had assumed the message meant: Candace You Loser, Bad Friendships Fail, Stacy. "That's what I thought it said. It's funny. I kind of thought you guys were avoiding me."

"Actually, *I* was trying to avoid you," a random guy suddenly added.

"Do I know you?" Candace asked him.

"Nope," he replied. "That's how great it's been working! Unknown guy is out. Peace!"

Candace and her friends frowned as the stranger walked away as mysteriously as he'd arrived. Then they started chatting excitedly about how they'd spend the rest of this beautiful summer day. Candace had to admit that as cool as it was to be crowned queen of Mars, it could never compare to an awesome afternoon hanging out with her friends!

And as for the Martians who'd lost their beloved queen, Candace was sure they'd get over it. After all, they'd managed for thousands of years without Candace; she figured they could get along pretty well until someone else crash-landed on their planet to lead them. At least she'd introduced them to music!

It turned out that the Martians didn't have

to wait that long for a new leader to appear. Just twenty-four hours later at the science fair, Mr. McGillicuddy overloaded the portal and sent Dr. Doofenshmirtz, a little girl's first-place-winning model volcano, *and* a mountain of broken volcano pieces right to Mars!

"Where am I?" Dr. Doofenshmirtz asked as he glanced around the red planet. Suddenly, a swarm of little green Martians surrounded him! "Okay. Be cool," Dr. Doofenshmirtz said nervously.

Then he realized that one of the Martians was carrying a gold crown, and a huge grin spread across his face. "Oh, you're going to make me your king?" he asked. "Well, okay, if you must!"

But the Martian walked right past Dr. Doofenshmirtz and approached the model volcano! To Dr. Doofenshmirtz's horror, the Martian placed the crown around the mouth of the volcano, and all the Martians cheered as they honored their new leader.

"What?" Dr. Doofenshmirtz exclaimed in outrage. "Oh, come on!"

But as all the Martians celebrated the first-place science project, it was time for Dr. Doofenshmirtz to face facts: when it came to competing against miniature model volcanoes, he was going to lose every time!

Don't miss the fun in the next
Phineas & Ferb book...

Off the Map

Adapted by Ellie O'Ryan
Based on the series created by Dan Povenmire & Jeff "Swampy" Marsh

The Flynn-Fletcher family van rumbled up the twisty mountain road, past pine trees and steep cliffs. Phineas and Ferb weren't worried, though. With their dad at the wheel, they were certain to stay five miles under the speed limit and follow proper driving procedures at all times.

"Hey, we're almost there!" Phineas said excitedly from the middle row of the van. He'd been looking forward to this trip since the very first day of summer vacation. It was a yearly tradition for his grandparents to invite Phineas,

Ferb, and all their friends to their mountain cabin for an amazing campout! From hiking through the woods to swimming in the lake, there was never a dull moment in the great outdoors. And since Phineas and Ferb wanted to make every minute of summer count, the campout fit in perfectly with their plans. So far, the stepbrothers' had been on one awesome adventure after another. And Phineas had a feeling that this camping trip was going to be legendary. He turned to one of his friends.

"What's the first thing you're going to do at camp, Buford?" he asked.

Buford didn't even have to think about it. "Find a nerd, take his underpants, and run 'em up the flagpole," he replied with a devious grin. As the resident bully of Danville, Buford had a knack for causing mischief in any situation.

Phineas winced. "How about you, Isabella?" he called over his shoulder to the girl sitting behind him.

Isabella smiled from her seat. "The Fireside Girls and I are going to work on our Accomplishment patches," she said.

"Accomplishment patches! Yay!" cheered a few other Fireside Girls, who popped up from the back of the van. Ferb jumped up, too, blowing on a squeaky whistle to add to the celebration. Everyone in the van was super-excited about going to camp!

Everyone—except for one person.

"How about you, sis?" Phineas asked his older sister, Candace, who was sitting across from him. "What's the first thing you're going to do at camp?"

"First of all, it's not 'camp,'" Candace corrected him. "It's just Grandma and Grandpa's cabin, and it's boring."

"But we made T-shirts!" Phineas exclaimed, holding up his blue custom Camp Phineas and Ferb shirt.

Candace continued as if her younger brother hadn't even spoken. "Secondly, I don't

like the outdoors, okay? I don't like bugs!"

Candace paused as she realized that Phineas was staring down at the floor of the van. "Phineas, are you even *listening* to me?" she snapped.

"I seem to have misplaced my ant farm," he replied thoughtfully.

"Mom!" Candace whined loudly.

"Yes, Candace?" their mother answered from the front seat, where she was reading a brochure.

"Do I *have* to go to Grandma and Grandpa's?" Candace sighed.

Candace's father looked back at her in the rearview mirror. "Oh, I think it's rather

sweet that Betty Joe and Grandpa Clyde invite you kids and all your friends every year," he said.

"But I'm not a kid!" Candace complained. "I'm a young adult. Can't I do something with you guys?"

"Of course you can, dear," her mom said excitedly. "You can join us at the antiques symposium. This year's keynote address will debate shellac versus lacquer."

"Woo-hoo!" her dad cried.

Candace sank back into her seat in defeat. "I'll take one of those shirts," she said with a sigh. After Phineas handed one to her, she started to cry into it. There was nothing else she could do, really—between Camp Phineas and Ferb and the antiques symposium, Candace was literally bored to tears!

Just a few miles away, Grandpa Clyde and Grandma Betty Joe waited in front of their cabin. Nestled in the wooded mountains, their tiny home sat near the banks of a freshwater lake and was surrounded by tall pine trees. It was truly the perfect place to enjoy the great outdoors!

Grandpa Clyde and Grandma Betty Joe stared expectantly down the dirt road leading up to the cabin.

"Where *are* they?" Grandpa Clyde asked in his croaky voice.

"Look! Oh, here they come now!" Grandma Betty Joe exclaimed happily.